For all the amazing children that have graced my life!

FOLLOW ME
TO
GOOD DREAMS

BY SHEA BIRNIE

ILLUSTRATIONS KAYLA OMSBERG

Hello,
I am the wizard,
Zippity-Zap.

I can make
good dreams happen
just like that!

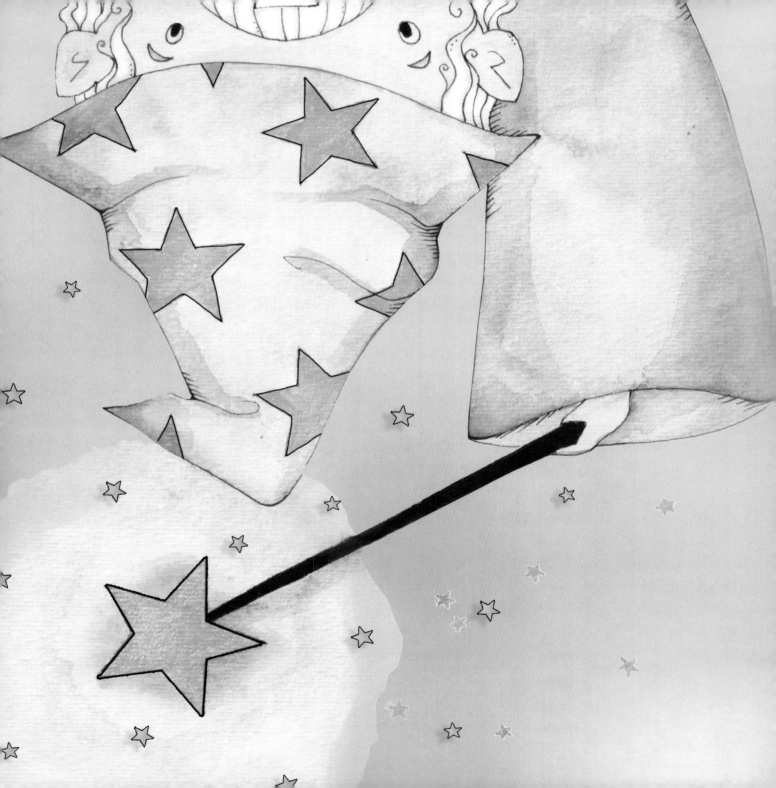

A wand, some good thoughts,
and a magic "tap, tap".
The strength is inside you,
make it happen in a...

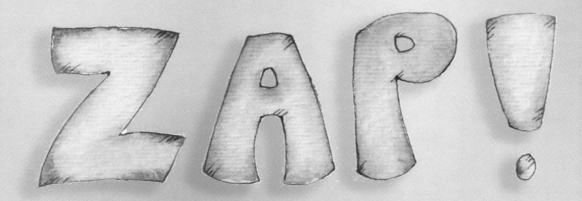

Lets make a list
that's just right for you.

Take a marker.
Write it down.
There are exciting
thoughts to
be found.

Happy Thoughts

1. ice cream! :) 🍦
2.
3.
4.
5.
6.
7.
8.
9.
10.
11.
12.

Here are a few
visions for you
tonight.

Something to think about
when you close
your eyes tight.

Running down the
beach with the sun
so bright.

Flying a wild
and wonderful
kite.

Being an
astronaut
rocketing
to the moon.

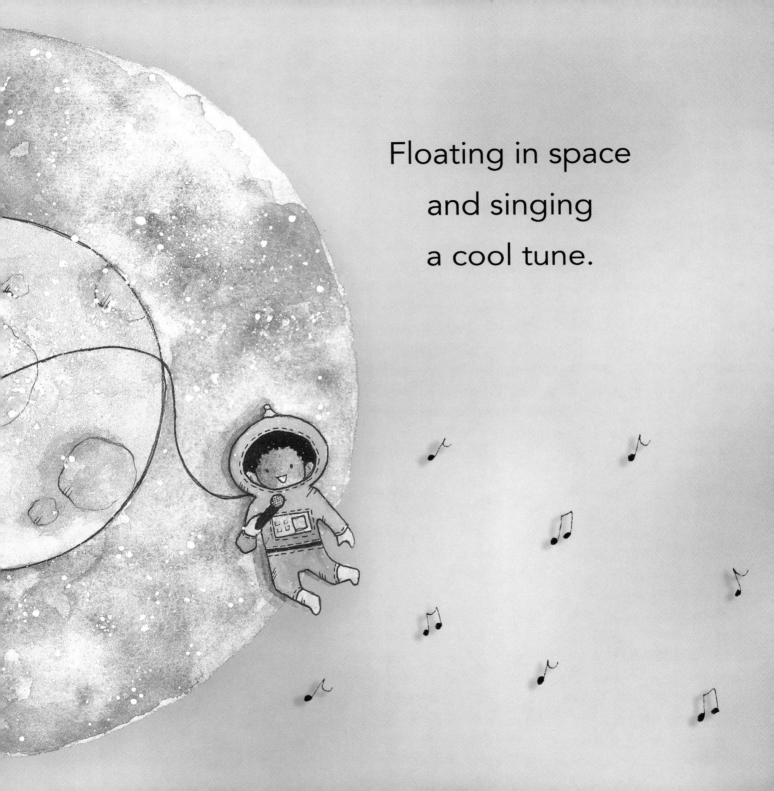

Floating in space
and singing
a cool tune.

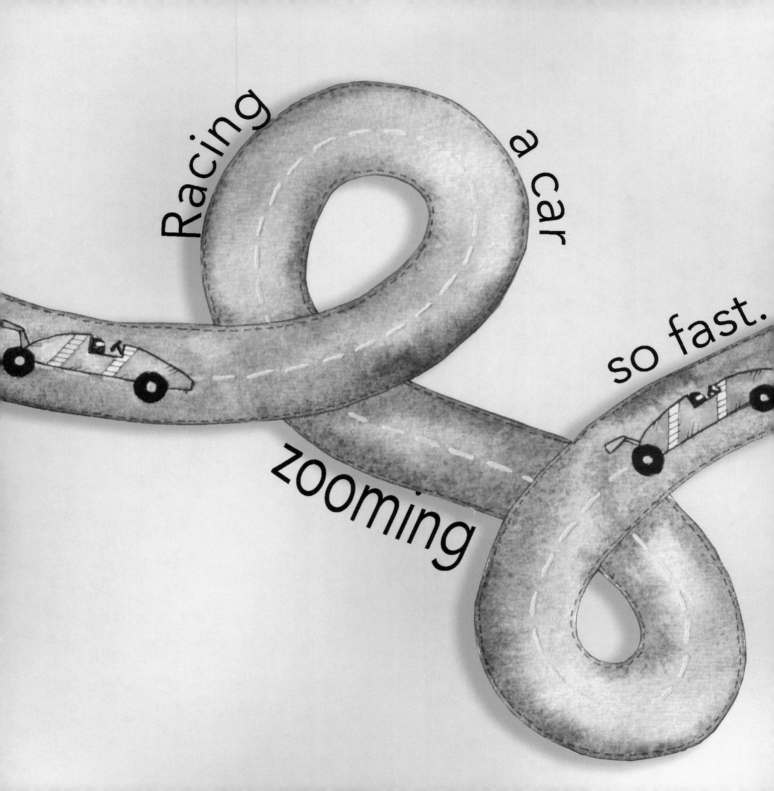

Racing a car zooming so fast.

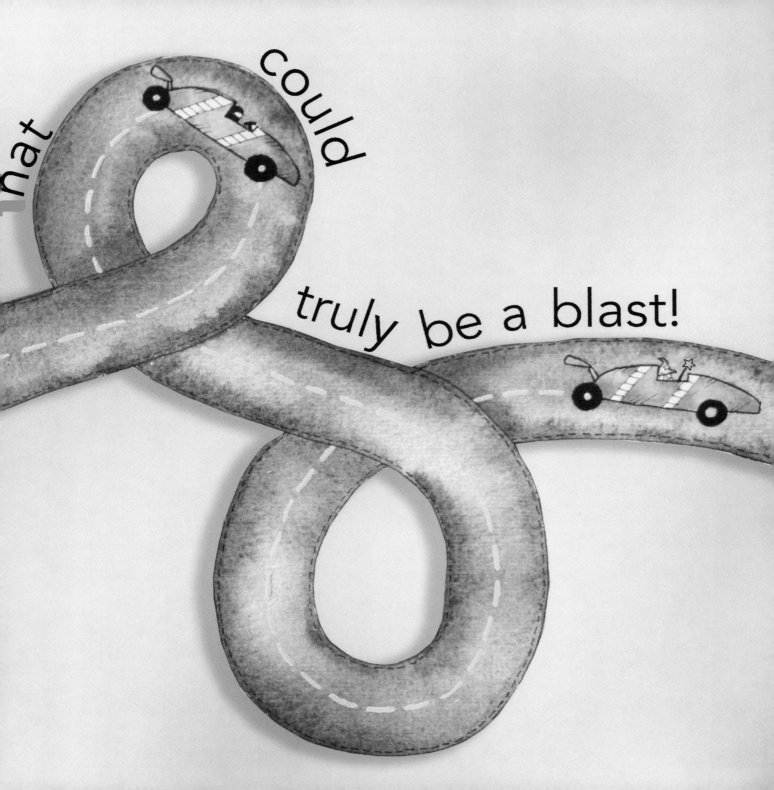

Thinking about
fun birthday
surprises.

With presents of many
shapes and sizes.

Being a brave knight
riding a dragon
in the sky.

Soaring through the universe,
flying so very high.

Dressing up
in costumes
for fun,

Trick or treat
for candies,
yum, yum!

Flying as a superhero,
here to save the day.

"Thank you! Thank you!" everyone would say.

Swimming
with
dolphins and
beautiful
fish.

That could
be your
greatest
wish.

Cuddling with family
just before bed.

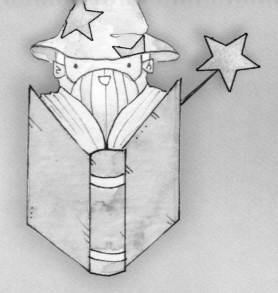

Reading, sharing,
resting head to head.

When you finish your thoughts,
when your list is done,

we'll be ready
for all kinds
of fun.

HAPPY LIST

Now read your list
LOUD and CLEAR,

Take three powerful
breaths without any fear.

Tap your wand
and swing it high.

Say your spell
and tell your
worries goodbye.

Rest your head lightly.

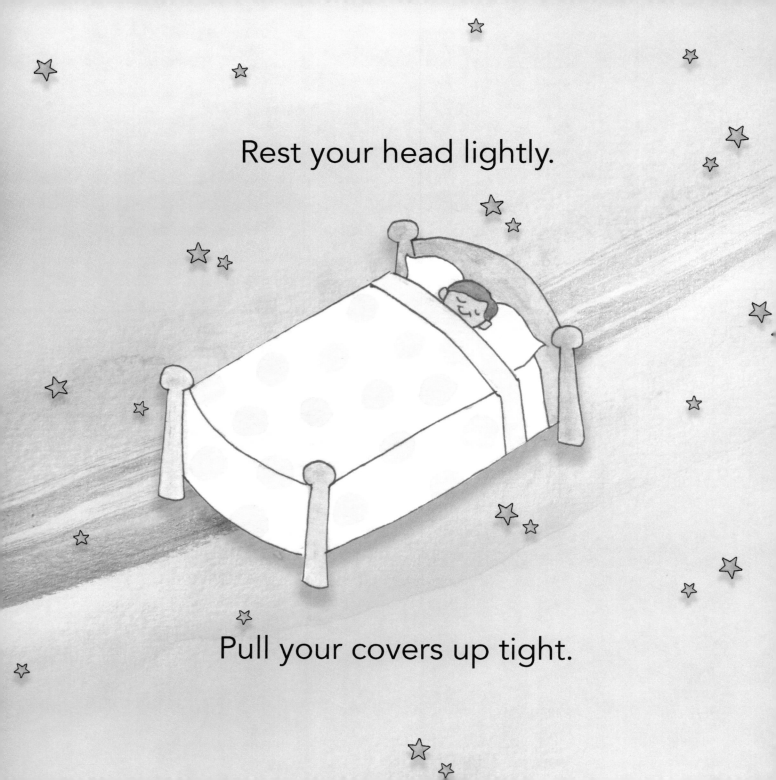

Pull your covers up tight.

Wonderful
dreams
await you
full of
magic and might.

HAPPY THOUGHTS

HAPPY THOUGHTS

HAPPY THOUGHTS

HAPPY THOUGHTS

HAPPY THOUGHTS

CPSIA information can be obtained at www.ICGtesting.com
Printed in the USA
BVIW12n0159091018
529667BV00010B/50